CHILDREN'S CLASSICS

The Railway Children

By
Edith Nesbitt

Adapted by
Mary Kerr

Edited by
Sophie Evans

Published by BK Books Ltd
First published in 2007
Copyright © BK Books Ltd

ISBN: 978-1-906068-49-3
Printed in China

Contents

Contents

Chapter 1

The Perfect Family

R oberta, Peter and Phyllis were just ordinary suburban children, who lived with their parents in a common red-brick house. They were not really railway children at all; in their minds, the train was just another mode of transportation, which they used when they went out of the city to enjoy their summer vacations.

Among all the children, Roberta, whom everyone called Bobbie, was the eldest.

Have you ever heard of a mother having a favorite amongst her children? Of course not! Mothers never have favorites, but if they did then Roberta would have been her mother's favorite. After Roberta, was Peter, who wished to be an engineer when he grew up. The youngest of all three was Phyllis.

In few words, they were a happy family. These three lucky children had everything they ever needed; pretty clothes, a lovely nursery with plenty of toys and a dog, whom they called James.

The children were blessed with loving parents. Unlike other mothers, their mother didn't spend her time playing cards or attending dull parties. She was always with her children, helping them in their lessons and playing games with them. She had a wonderful talent for writing stories and short, funny poems, which she read aloud during tea-time! Whether it was a grand occasion, like a birthday, or a 'small' occasion, like the christening of the new kittens, or the refurbishing of the doll's house, it was always accompanied by a 'short poem'. They also had a father who was just perfect—never cross, never unjust, and always ready to play with them. As far as the children were concerned, they had the PERFECT PARENTS.

Everything was perfect at home, till the dreadful day came. It was Peter's tenth birthday. Among other presents, Peter received a model engine that appeared almost real. But its charm lasted for only three days. Whether it was Peter's inexperience in handling the engine, or Phyllis' mishandling, the engine suddenly went off with a BANG!

Peter's feelings were terribly injured. The others said he cried over the loss, but of course, boys of ten do not cry, however great a tragedy hits them. He said that his eyes were red because he had a cold, and this turned out to be true. Peter stayed in bed the next day. Mother was worried by his behavior; she thought that he might have measles. But her fears disappeared when he said, "I hate gruel, I hate barley water and I hate bread and milk. I want to get up and have something *real* to eat."

"What would you like?" she asked.

"Pigeon pie," Peter said, eagerly, "a *very* LARGE pigeon pie." Therefore, a large pigeon pie was prepared for him and he savored every mouthful.

To please Peter, everyone tried to fix up the engine but no one was able to accomplish the task. Now, all their hopes rested on their father. The children believed that their father could mend anything; he had often acted as a veterinary surgeon to their wooden rocking horse. Once, he had saved its life, when even the carpenter had given up! Father had been away in the country for three or four days and would be arriving home that night. The children eagerly awaited his return.

Mother had told Peter that it would be a good idea to be unselfish and not tell father about the problem till he had rested a bit. It was difficult for a young boy to be so patient but Peter followed his mother's advice and waited for his father to finish his dinner.

At last, mother said to father, "Now dear, if you are quite comfortable, we want to tell you about the great railway accident and ask your advice." "All right," said father, "fire away!"

And so, Peter narrated the sad tale and fetched what remained of the engine.

"Hmm!" said father, after he had inspected the damaged engine. The children held their breath and looked at him expectantly.

"Is there no hope?" Peter asked in a low and trembling voice.

"Hope? Of course there is. And a lot of hope indeed," said father, cheerfully. "It just needs some solder and a new valve. I will mend it on Saturday, when all of you can help me."

The discussion continued until there was a knock at the front door. Ruth, the parlor maid, came in to say, "Sir, two gentlemen want to see you. I've shown them into the library."

"Do hurry back dear," mother whispered as he went in the direction of the library.

However, this didn't happen. Mother tried to make good use of the time by

telling the children a fairy tale of a princess who had green eyes. But it was difficult to hold their attention as the loud voices could be heard through the library door and father's voice was the loudest. Then, the bell rang and everyone heaved a sigh of relief.

"They must be going now," Phyllis said.

The children were expecting father to enter the room, but instead, Ruth came in, agitated.

"Please ma'am," she said, "the master wants you to come into the study. He is looking dreadful; I think he's had some bad news. Madam, be prepared for the worst."

"That'll do, Ruth," mother said gently, "you can go."

Mother went into the library, and there were more noises. Then the bell rang again and Ruth was asked to fetch a cab. The children heard people walk out and the cab drive away. They sensed that all was not well when they heard the front door shut. The mother walked into the room with her face as white as snow; her eyes were large and shining with tears. Without narrating anything about the outside event, she said, "It's bedtime," her voice hardly above a whisper. "Today, Ruth will put you to bed."

"But you promised we would sit up late tonight because father has come home," Phyllis said.

"Father has been called away on some urgent business," mother said. "Come darlings, don't trouble me, go at once to sleep." The children kissed their dear mother, wished her a good night and left.

Roberta gave her mother an extra hug and whispered, "Was it, indeed, bad news? What happened mummy, why are you sad?"

"I can't tell you anything tonight, my dear. Go, dear, go *now*." So, Roberta left too, along with Phyllis and Peter.

Late that night, mother came up and kissed all three children as they lay asleep. Roberta was the only one who was awakened by this kiss. But she lay on the bed as still as a mouse and said nothing. 'If mother doesn't want us to know why she's been crying,' she told herself as she heard her mother weep, 'we *won't* know it. That's all.'

The next morning, when they came down for breakfast, they were surprised to see mother not present at the breakfast table.

"Where has mother gone?" Phyllis asked.

"To London," Ruth said abruptly.

"Something awful must have happened, which our parents don't want to share with us," said Peter.

They had their breakfast in silence and left for school. When they returned at one o'clock, for lunch, mother was still not at home. She remained absent at teatime also. It was nearly seven when she came in and sank into an armchair. She looked so ill and tired that the children decided not trouble her with their questions.

After a cup of tea, mother said, "Now my darlings, I want to tell you something. The men who were here last night, did bring some bad news and father will be away for some time. I am very worried. I want you all to help me and not make things more difficult. You can help me just by being good and not quarrelling whenever I'm away."

"We won't quarrel," said all three unanimously.

And from that day, when Roberta, Peter and Phyllis said something, they meant it.

"Then," mother went on, "I want one more favor from you: please don't ask me anything about the trouble we are going through."

After a pause, she continued, "It isn't necessary for you to know anything about it, as it is related to business, and you are too young to understand business."

Roberta was not as young as her mother thought her to be. "Mother, is it something to do with the government?" she asked, for father was in a government office.

"Yes," mother said. "Now, it's bedtime my darlings. And don't you worry. It's going to be all right in the end."

"Then *you* should also not worry, mother," Phyllis said, "and we'll all be as good as gold."

Mother sighed and kissed them good night.

"I say," Phyllis said, once they were alone, "you used to say that it's so dull, nothing happens, like in our story books. Now something *has* happened."

"But I never wanted such things to happen that would make mother so unhappy," Roberta said sadly.

Chapter 2

The Three Chimneys

For some weeks, the atmosphere of the house remained horrid. Mother was always out, occupied with certain troubles. Mealtimes had also become dull. To make matters worse, Aunt Emma came on a visit. She was much older than mother and believed in keeping children in their proper places. The children thought that a 'proper place' was anywhere where they could see as little of Aunt Emma as possible.

13

The children preferred to pass their time with the servants, rather than Aunt Emma. The servants tried to amuse them. The Cook, if in a good mood, would sing comic songs. However, the servants never told the children what bad news the gentlemen had brought with them.

One day, when mother came home, she went straight to bed. She stayed there for two days. The doctor came, and the children crept miserably about the house and wondered if the world was coming to an end. It was three days later when mother came down to join them for breakfast. She appeared very pale and there were lines on her face.

She gave a weak smile and said, "Now my darlings, everything is settled. We're going to leave this house and go and live in a beautiful, little white house in the country. I know you'll love it."

When you go for a short trip, you simply pack a few clothes. But it was not a vacation

they were planning; therefore, furniture, books, boxes and all sorts of things were packed. The children enjoyed it very much. All of their beds had gone. A bed was made up for Peter, on the drawing room sofa.

"I say, this is great," he said, tossing and turning joyously, as mother tucked him in. "I do like moving! I wish we moved once a month."

"But I don't like it!" she laughed.

"Good night, Peter dear," mother said.

As she turned away, Roberta saw her face. She would never forget that grief stricken face. 'Oh, mother!' she whispered to herself as she got into bed. 'How brave you are! Who can be brave enough to laugh when surrounded by so many troubles? Mother, I want to be like you. I love you so much!'

The next day lots and lots of boxes were filled. Then, late in the afternoon, a cab came to take them to the station. Aunt Emma saw them off. At first they enjoyed looking out of the window, but as evening descended, they grew more and more sleepy. They were awakened by their Mother's gentle shaking and saying, "Wake up, dears. We are here."

They woke up, cold and melancholy and stood shivering on the draughty platform while their luggage was taken off the train and loaded onto a cart. They watched miserably as the engine pulled out, puffing and blowing, till it disappeared into the darkness.

This was the first time in their lives that they had witnessed the railway so closely. But they were unaware of the fact that the railway would soon become the center of their lives! They only shivered and sneezed and hoped that the walk to the new house would not be long. Peter's nose was colder than ever and Phyllis' shoelaces had come undone as usual.

"Come," mother said, "we've got to walk. There aren't any cabs here. The cart loaded with our luggage will follow us behind."

The walk was dark and muddy. The children stumbled a little on the rough road, and Phyllis absent-mindedly fell into a puddle. She was picked up, very unhappy. "It's a long walk, mother said, "There's the house. I wonder why she's shut the windows!"

"Who's *she*?" asked Roberta.

"The woman I've employed to clean the place, put the furniture straight and get supper."

There was a low wall and tall trees.

"That's the garden," mother said.

There was no light in any of the windows. Everyone knocked on the door, but no one answered.

The man who drove their cart said, "You see, your train was late, so she must have left for home."

"But how can she leave? She's got the keys to the house," mother said.

"Oh, she might have left them under the doormat," said the cart-man; "we do that a lot around here."

He took the lantern off his cart and stooped.

"Look, here it is," he said and unlocked the door with the keys. He set the lantern on the table.

"Do you know where we can find a candle?" he asked.

"I don't know where anything is," mother replied quite cheerlessly.

The cart-man struck a match and lighted a candle, which he found on the table.

By its thin little glimmer, the children were able to see a large, bare kitchen with a stone floor. The kitchen table stood in the middle of the room and the chairs were placed in one corner. The pots, pans, brooms and crockery were stacked up in another. There was no fire, only cold, dead ashes in the fireplace! What a contrast this place was to the children of the red brick house.

Just as the cart-man turned to go, after bringing in the boxes, they all heard a rustling sound, which seemed to come from inside the walls of the house.

The children were quite afraid.

"Oh, what's that?" cried the girls.

"It's only the rats," the cart-man shouted over his back, as he drove away.

A sudden gush of air blew out the candle.

"Oh dear, I wish we hadn't come!" Phyllis said, as she knocked a chair over.

"It's only the rats!" Peter exclaimed, in the dark.

"What fun!" mother said, feeling for the matches on the table. She struck a match and lighted the candle and everyone looked at each other.

"Well, you've often wanted something to happen and now it has. Isn't it quite an adventure? I told Mrs. Viney to have supper ready. I suppose she's laid it in the dining room. Let's go and check."

The dining room opened out from the kitchen. Sure enough, there was the table and the chairs, but supper couldn't be seen anywhere.

"Let's investigate the other rooms," mother said.

In each room, there was the same kind of half-arranged furniture but nothing to eat.

"What a strange old woman!" mother said. "She's just walked off with the money and not left us anything to eat."

"So will we not be having supper at all? Will we be going to bed hungry?" asked Phyllis, dismayed.

"Oh no, dear," mother said, "we will have our supper, only it'll mean unpacking one of those big boxes."

The children got busy in unpacking one of the big boxes. After a lot of hitting and hammering, the box opened.

"Hurrah!" mother exclaimed. "Here are some candles! You girls go and light them."

"How many shall we light?" asked Phyllis.

"As many as you like," mother said, with a smile. "The most important thing is to be cheerful. Nobody can be cheerful in the dark except owls and dormice."

That evening, the fourteen candles were lighted in the dining room. To fight the cold, Roberta rushed to fetch coal and wood to light a fire. The fire and candles gave a cheerful look to the dining room and the girls hastily tidied the room.

"Bravo!" cried mother, coming in with a tray full of things. "I'll just get a tablecloth and then we can have our supper."

Mother got the tablecloth and then a real feast was laid out on it. Everyone was tired, but their weariness flew away at the sight of the funny and delightful supper. There were biscuits, the Marie and the plain kind, sardines, preserved ginger, cooking raisins, candied peel and marmalade.

"We should be grateful to Aunt Emma, who packed up all the odds and ends from the store cupboard," mother said.

"Let's drink to Aunt Emma's health," Roberta said, suddenly. "We would have slept hungry, if she hadn't packed all this stuff. Here's to Aunt Emma!" They all drank the ginger wine and water. All of them realized that they had been a little hard on Aunt Emma.

After dinner, they quickly made their beds. "Good night," mother said. "I'm sure there aren't any rats, but I'll leave my door open. If a mouse does come, just scream. I'll come and tell it exactly what I think of it."

Mother's assurance helped the children go off to sleep immediately.

The next morning, Roberta woke up Phyllis, by pulling her hair gently.

"What's the matter?" asked Phyllis, still half asleep.

"Wake up! Wake up!" Roberta said. "We're in the new house, don't you remember? There are no servants to look after the house chores. Get up! We should make the house beautiful before mother wakes up."

By the time they got dressed, Peter, too, was ready. There was no water in their room, so they went to the pump in the yard. They washed as much as they thought was necessary; one pumped and the other washed. It was splashy but interesting.

"It's much more fun than washing in a basin," remarked Roberta.

"This is far, far prettier than our red-brick house," declared Phyllis. "Let's go in and begin the work."

They lighted the fire, put the kettle on, and arranged the crockery for breakfast, though they could not find all the right things. After they did everything they could do, they went out again to enjoy the fresh, bright morning.

It was a hilly country side. Down the hill, they could see the railway line and the black, yawning mouth of a tunnel, though the station was out of sight. There was a great bridge with tall arches, which ran across one end of the valley. The children sat down on a great flat gray stone that had pushed itself up out of the grass.

At eight o'clock, when mother came out to look for them, she found them fast asleep.

They had made an excellent fire and had placed the kettle on it at about half past five. By eight, the fire had been out for some time, the water had all boiled away and the bottom of the kettle was burned out.

Unlike other mothers, their mother was not angry with them, as she knew that they were only trying to help her. She then led them into the room which they had mistaken, the previous night, for a cabinet. The children could not believe their eyes. Before them, on a table, lay a magnificent feast; there was cold roast beef, with bread, butter, cheese and a pie.

"Pie for breakfast!" cried Peter.

"Well, this is the supper we ought to have had last night!" mother said. Along with the lovely spread, there was a note from Mrs. Viney. It explained that she had to go home early as her son-in-law had broken his arm, but that she would be back, at ten o'clock, today.

For the children, the meal was a wonderful treat and they loved every bit of it!

"You see, it's more like dinner than breakfast to us, because we were up so early," Peter said, passing his plate for more.

The day passed in helping mother to unpack and arrange things in the house. Six small legs quite ached with running about, while their owners carried clothes, crockery and all sorts of things to their proper places.

It was not till quite late in the afternoon when mother said, "Thank you children, for helping me. That'll do for today." Once mother said so, all of them had just one question.

"Where shall we go now?"

"To the railway station," was the unanimous cry. And off they went.

Chapter 3

The Coal Mining

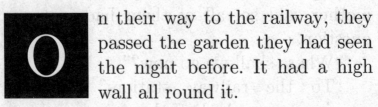n their way to the railway, they passed the garden they had seen the night before. It had a high wall all round it.

The track leading to the railway line was all downhill. It was covered with smooth turf and strewn with gray and yellow rocks. It ended in a steep run and a wooden fence. They all climbed up onto the fence and there, before them, was the railway with shining metals, telegraph wires, posts and signals. Suddenly, their attention was caught by a rumbling sound that made them look along the line to the right. The dark mouth of the tunnel appeared like a yawn on the face of the rocky cliff. The next moment, a train came out of the tunnel, shrieking and snorting, as it passed them.

"Oh!" Roberta said, drawing a long breath. "It was like a great dragon rushing past. Did you feel its hot wings fan us?"

Peter said, "I never thought that seeing a train from so near would be such a breathtaking experience. It's the most ripping sport!"

"I wonder if that train is going to London," said Roberta.

"We can find out from the station; let's go!" said Peter. They walked along the edge of the line and heard the telegraph wires buzzing over their heads.

It was after a long walk that they reached the station. Never before had any of them been to a station without a grown-up, so it felt like a great adventure.

They peeped into the porters' room. There was a lone porter and he was fast asleep behind a newspaper. There were a great many lines crossing at the station, with some of them ending abruptly in the station yard. On one side of the yard, there was a great heap of coal. It looked like a solid building, built of large, square blocks of coal. There was a line of whitewash painted right to the top of the coal wall.

The porter came out at the sound of the station gong and Peter asked him, "Sir, can you please tell me what the white mark on the coal stands for?"

"To mark how much coal is there, so that we can immediately know if anyone has stolen any," replied the porter.

Peter did not think about it much at the time, but it remained at the back of his mind.

Peter also asked the porter about the destination of the train they had watched leaving the tunnel. It was, indeed, heading for London. The three of them walked along the lines for a while before returning home.

* * * *

Ever since father had gone away, mother had been sad. The children soon got used to the absence of their father and although they missed him terribly, they never expressed it before their mother. They also got used to not going to school and seeing very little of their mother. She spent almost all her day shut up in her room upstairs, writing, writing and writing. She joined them only at tea time, when, at the table, she read aloud the stories she had written. Gradually, the

memories of their life at the red-brick house began to fade away.

The economic condition of the family was not sound. Mother had tried to convey this truth to the children. She had told them more than once that they were 'quite poor now', but the children didn't feel much of a difference in their lives.

It was the month of June and it rained heavily for three days. The weather turned very cold. The children went up to their mother's room and knocked at the door.

"Well, what is it?" asked mother from inside.

"Mother," said Roberta, "may we light a fire?"

Mother answered, "No my dear. We can't afford a fire in the month of June. Coal is so expensive. If you are cold, go and play in the attic. That'll warm you. Now run along, I'm very busy!"

"These days, Mother's always busy," Phyllis whispered to Peter.

Peter did not answer. He shrugged his shoulders. He was thinking.

However, they all went up to the attic to play.

That same evening, at tea, when Phyllis was about to add jam to her bread and butter, mother said, "Choose one, jam or butter my dear, not jam *and* butter. We can't afford that sort of luxury nowadays." Phyllis finished the slice of bread and butter in silence.

During tea time, Peter was lost in his own thoughts. After tea, he said to his sisters, "I have an idea."

"What's that?" they asked impatiently. "I am not going to tell you," was Peter's unexpected reply.

"Oh, very well," said Roberta. "We are not interested in your silly ideas anyway."

"But you'll know of it some day," said Peter, trying not to lose his temper. "The only reason I won't tell you my idea now is because it may be wrong and I don't want to pull you into it."

"If it's something wrong, don't dare to try it Peter. I don't want you to create any trouble," said Roberta. "Let me do it instead of you."

But Phyllis said, "If you are going to do wrong, I should like to do it too!"

"No," Peter said, quite touched by this devotion. "All I want you to do is to keep my disappearance a secret from mother."

Two evenings after this conversation took place, Peter called the girls.

"Come with me," he said, "and bring the Roman Chariot."

The Roman Chariot was a very old perambulator that was in the loft.

"Follow your chief," Peter said, and led the way down the hill. Phyllis and Roberta followed him.

He came to the huge coal wall, which they had seen a few days back. Peter said, "Here's the first coal from the St. Peter's Mine. We'll take it home in the chariot."

At first, the chariot was packed full with coal. However, it was too heavy for the children to wheel uphill. So it had to be partially unpacked again! They had to make three trips to carry the coal from Peter's mine to mother's cellar.

The children's trip to the coal mine continued. A week later, Mrs. Viney remarked to mother how well the last lot of coal was holding out. When the children heard this, they were more than happy. They hugged each other and struggled hard to stop themselves from revealing the secret.

Soon, they all stopped wondering about whether taking the coal had been wrong. But then came a dreadful night when the stationmaster crept out very quietly to the yard and waited like a cat by a mouse hole. Soon, he saw something small and dark scrabbling on the top of the heap. He waited till the thing was within his reach, then his hand pounced on the small thing; it was, of course, Peter. He had an old carpenter's bag full of coal in his small hands.

"So I've succeeded in catching you, you young thief," said the stationmaster.

"I'm not a thief," Peter said, as confidently as he could. "I'm a coal-miner."

"Shut up and come along to the station," said the stationmaster.

"Oh no," cried a distressed voice in the darkness, "please, not the police station!"

"Let him go," said another voice from the darkness. "Can't you decide, here and now, what you'll do to us? We are as much at fault as Peter is. We helped him in carrying the coal away and we knew where he got it."

"No, you didn't," Peter said.

"Yes, we did," said Roberta. "We knew it all the time, we only pretended that we didn't."

"Don't hold me!" Peter said. "I won't run away."

The stationmaster loosened Peter's collar, struck a match and looked at them by its flickering light.

"Why!" he exclaimed. "Are you not the children from the Three Chimneys up there? Tell me now, what made you steal?"

"I didn't think I was stealing. If I had taken the coal out from the sides then it would have been stealing, but I dug it out from the middle. So I had to *mine* it," Peter said indignantly.

"So, you did all this for fun?" asked the stationmaster.

"Oh, you think we would carry such a heavy cart uphill, just for fun?" Peter asked.

"Then why *did* you?" The stationmaster's voice was kinder now.

"You remember that rainy day?" Peter replied. "Well, that day when we were feeling cold, mother said that coal was really expensive so we couldn't afford a fire. We always had fire when it was cold at our other house, and..."

"Well," said the stationmaster, thoughtfully, "I will let you go this time, but remember, stealing is stealing, whether you call it mining or whether you don't. Now run along home."

"Do you mean you aren't going to punish us? Well, you are a brick!" Peter said with enthusiasm.

"You're a dear!" Roberta said.

"You're a darling!" Phyllis chipped in.

"That's fine," said the stationmaster.

And on this note, they parted and ran uphill to the Three Chimneys.

Chapter 4

Mother's Illness

E ven after the trouble of Peter's coal mining, the children could not keep away from the railway. They knew the hours when certain trains passed and they gave names to them. The 9.15 UP was called the 'Green Dragon.' The 10.07 DOWN was the 'Worm of Wantley.' The Midnight Town Express, whose shrieking sometimes woke them up, was the 'Fearsome Fly-By-Night.' Peter had named it on the spot one night, after its loud shrieking noise woke him up.

It was by the 'Green Dragon' that the old gentleman traveled. He was a very nice-looking old gentleman. He had a fresh collar, clean-shaven face, white hair and he wore a

top hat that was different from the kind the others wore. Of course, the children didn't see all this at first. In fact, the first thing they noticed about the old gentleman was his hand.

It happened one morning, as they sat on the fence waiting for the 'Green Dragon'. It was three and a quarter minutes late by Peter's Waterbury watch.

"The Green Dragon is going to meet father," Phyllis said. "If it were really a real dragon, we could stop it and ask it to take our love to father. I wonder why father doesn't even write to us."

"Mother says he's been too busy," Roberta answered, "but he'll write soon."

"I have an idea," Phyllis suggested. "Let's all wave to the 'Green Dragon' as it goes by. If it's a magic dragon, it'll understand and take our love to father. And if it isn't, three waves aren't much. We shall never miss them."

So when the 'Green Dragon' came out of the tunnel, all three children stood on the railing and waved their pocket-handkerchiefs. In response to them, a hand with a newspaper waved back. It was the old gentleman's hand. After this, it became the custom to exchange waves between the children and the 9.15 train.

Mother, all this time, was very busy with her writing. She would send her stories to the editors and whenever an editor selected her story, she would treat the children with buns.

One day, when Peter was going down to the village to get buns for tea, he met the stationmaster. Peter felt very uncomfortable, for he had by now realized that his 'coal mining' was less of mining and more of stealing. He did not wish to greet the stationmaster, so he tried to pass unnoticed.

It was the stationmaster who wished 'good morning' as he passed by. Peter answered,

"Good morning." Then he thought, 'Perhaps he didn't recognize me, or he would not be so polite.'

And then, before he knew what he was doing, he ran up to the stationmaster and said, "I don't want you to be polite to me if you don't know who I am."

"Eh?" said the stationmaster.

"You have forgotten, when you said good morning, that it was me who took the coals," said Peter.

"Why," said the stationmaster, "I wasn't thinking anything about the coals. Let bygones be bygones. You may visit us at the station whenever you want."

"Thank you," Peter said, "I'm glad that you have excused me. The stationmaster left with this and Peter continued on to get the buns.

The next day, when they had sent their love to their father by the 'Green Dragon', Peter proudly led the way to the station. Roberta and Phyllis did not want to go, but

when Peter told them about his meeting with the stationmaster and the invitation, the girls agreed to accompany him.

"Stop a minute, my bootlace is undone again," cried out Phyllis on the way.

"It is *always* undone," Peter said. Phyllis did up her bootlace and they went on in silence. They reached the station and spent two happy hours with the porter. They became good friends and he told them many things that they had not known before—for instance, the things that hook carriages together are called couplings; the pipes that hang like great serpents over the couplings are meant to stop the train.

"If you can get hold of one of them when the train is going and pull them apart," he said, "she'd stop dead with a jerk."

"Who's *she*?" Phyllis asked.

"The train, of course," replied the porter, and from that day on the train was never again 'IT' to the children.

The children had a delightful conversation with the porter and did not realize how the time had flown by so quickly. The stationmaster came out once or twice and was pleased to see them.

"Just as if the coal mining had never been discovered," Phyllis whispered to her sister.

The stationmaster promised to take them up into the signal-box one of these days, when he was not too busy. That evening, they told mother all about the railway, the porter and the stationmaster.

"I'm so glad you like the railway. But you must promise me that you will not walk on the line," said mother.

"Mother, didn't *you* ever walk on the railway lines when you were little?" asked Phyllis.

"Yes, but darlings you don't know how fond I am of you. What would I do if you got hurt?" replied mother.

It was the very next day that mother had to stay in bed because her head ached and her hands burned hot. She could not eat anything, and had a sore throat.

In the evening, Peter went to fetch the doctor. The doctor's name was W. W. Forrest and he came at once. He talked to Peter on the way back. He seemed a charming man. When he had seen mother, he said it was influenza and that she would soon be fine.

"I suppose you'll want to be head-nurse," said Doctor Forrest to Roberta. "Well, I'll have some medicine sent down. Give her some beef-tea once the fever goes down."

He wrote down a list, but when Roberta showed it to her mother, she laughed.

"Nonsense," said mother, lying in bed. "I can't afford all this rubbish."

Roberta went downstairs and told Phil and Peter what the doctor had said, and their mother's response. "And now," she said, "we have to do something. We must find out some way to get all of the things the doctor said. Now both of you think as hard as you can," Roberta said, frowning.

Well, they did come up with a brilliant idea. When Roberta had gone up to sit with mother, the other two got busy with scissors, a white sheet, a paintbrush and a pot of black paint. They messed up the first sheet, so they took another out of the linen cupboard.

Mother had not recovered from her illness and she kept muttering to herself in her sleep. Early next morning, Roberta heard her name and, jumping out of bed, she ran to her mother's bedside.

"Oh–ah, yes, I think I was asleep," mother said. "My dear, I hate to give you all this trouble. I shall be all right in a day or two."

"Yes," Roberta said and tried to smile.

Roberta's eyes were sore with lack of sleep, but she tidied the room and arranged everything neatly before the doctor came. It was around half past eight when the doctor knocked at the door.

"Everything fine, little nurse?" he asked. "Did you get all the things I prescribed?"

"I've got the brandy; we will get the tea and the beef soon." Roberta said.

"The head-nurse should take care of herself. Mrs. Viney will sit with your mother, you go straight to bed and sleep till dinner-time," said the nice doctor.

That morning, when the 9.15 came out of the tunnel, the old gentleman in the first-class carriage got ready to wave his hand to the three children on the fence. Today, only Peter was there. He pointed to a large white sheet nailed against the fence. On the sheet there were thick black letters more than a foot long. The words were—*LOOK OUT AT THE STATION.*

The old gentleman looked out and, at first, he saw nothing unusual. It was only just as the train was beginning to puff and start again that he saw Phyllis. She was running with the train. "Oh," she said, "I thought I'd missed you. My bootlaces would keep coming out and I fell over them twice. Here, take it."

With these words, she thrust a warm, dampish letter into his hand as the train moved.

The old man opened the letter, which read, "Dear Mr. 'We-do-not-know-your-name,'

Mother is ill and the doctor says to give her the things mentioned at the end of the letter, but we can't afford them. You are the only person we know here. Father is away and we do not know the address. He will pay you, or, if he has lost all his money, Peter will pay you when he is a man. We promise it on our honor. Please give the parcel to the stationmaster. Say it is for Peter who was sorry about the coals. He will know.

Roberta, Peter and Phyllis."

Then, came the list of things the doctor had ordered. The old gentleman went through it once more and his eyebrows went up. He had read it thrice before putting it in his pocket.

At about six that evening, there was a knock at the backdoor.

The children rushed to open it, and there stood the friendly porter, with a big packet in his hands.

"The old gentleman asked me to fetch it up right away," he said.

"Thank you very much," Peter said.

"I am sorry your mother is not well. I've also brought her a bit of sweetbrier."

The porter left after talking to the children for a while.

The children impatiently undid the packet. All the things they had asked for were there. There were also a good many things they had not asked for, like peaches, port wine, two chickens, and a cardboard box of big red roses with long stalks. There was a letter too. It read,

"Dear Roberta, Phyllis and Peter,

I am sending you the things you wanted. Your mother will want to know where they came from. Tell her a friend, who heard she was unwell, sent them. When she gets well, you must tell her all about it. And if she says you ought not to have asked for the things, tell her that I say you were quite right to do so, and that it was my pleasure to have this opportunity.

G. P."

"I think we *were* right," Phyllis said.

"Right? Of course we were right," Roberta said.

"But at the same time, I don't know how we will tell all of this to mother," said Peter, with his hands in his pockets.

Chapter 5

Roberta's Birthday

ith the kind gentleman's help, mother soon regained her health. The children thought to thank their friend for his kindness, so they displayed a banner with the following message,

'*She Is Nearly Well. Thank You –To The 'Green Dragon.*'

The old gentleman read it, and waved, cheerfully, from the train.

The children realized that it was time to

tell their mother about the old gentleman.
It was not an easy task, nevertheless they
did it. Mother was extremely angry. She was
angrier than they had ever known her to be.
It became worse when she suddenly began to
cry. All at once everyone found themselves
taking part in a crying party.

Mother stopped first. She dried
her eyes and said, "I'm sorry I was so
angry."

"We didn't mean to trouble you,
mummy," sobbed Roberta.

Peter and Phyllis sniffed in unison.

"Now, listen," mother said, "it's quite
true that we're poor. But you mustn't go
telling everyone about our condition. It's
not right. And you must never, ever ask
strangers for help."

They all hugged her and promised that
they would never do it again.

"Now I'll write a letter to your old
gentleman, and thank him for his kindness,"
said mother.

So, she wrote a letter to the old gentleman and the children took it down to the stationmaster. Then, they went to the porter's room. He told them that his name was Perks and that he was married with three children. It was on this day that the children learned that not all engines were alike. The children agreed, as they went home that evening, that the porter was a nice man.

The next day was Roberta's twelfth birthday. She was out in the garden, all alone. That day, the others remained aloof as they prepared for her birthday surprise. Now that she was alone, she had time to think. She thought about what her mother had said when she was down with the fever.

"Oh, what a doctor's bill there'll be for this!" her mother had muttered.

Roberta's mind remained occupied with the thought of the doctor's bill. Then suddenly, she made up her mind. She went out of the garden and walked along until she came to the bridge that crossed the canal and led to the village and here she waited. Presently, she heard the sound of wheels. It was the doctor's dogcart.

He stopped and called out, "Hello head-nurse! Want a lift?"

"I wanted to meet you," Roberta said.

"I hope your mother is well," said the doctor.

"Yes, but…"

"Well, hop in then and we'll go for a drive."

Roberta climbed in and the brown horse was made to turn round.

"This is wonderful," Roberta said, as the dogcart flew along the road by the canal.

"Now, tell me, what's the trouble?" asked the doctor.

Roberta fiddled with the hook of the driving apron.

"Come on, tell me," goaded the doctor.

"It's really hard to tell, because of what mother said." Roberta said.

"What *did* your mother say?" inquired the doctor.

"She said I should not tell everyone that we are poor. But you aren't everyone, are you?" asked Roberta.

"Not at all," said the doctor, cheerfully.

"Well, I know doctors are very expensive. Mrs. Viney told me that her doctoring only cost her two pence a week because she belongs to a club. She told me all about it."

"Yes?"

"Can't we also join the club like Mrs. Viney?"

The doctor was silent.

"You aren't angry with me, are you?" Roberta asked, in a very small voice.

"Angry? How could I be? You're such a sensible little woman. You shouldn't worry. I'll make things all right for your mother, even if I have to make a special club just for her. And, remember, you aren't to worry about doctor's bills or you'll be ill yourself," said the doctor.

When Roberta parted from the doctor at the top of the field, she was happy that the doctor had promised to help her.

Roberta had just enough time to dress herself, before the bell rang. "There," Phyllis said, coming to her. "That's to announce that the surprise is ready."

Roberta went into the dining room, feeling shy. When she opened the door, she found herself standing in a new world, which was filled with lights, flowers and music. Mother, Peter and Phyllis were standing in a row at the end of the table. There were twelve candles on the table, one for each of Roberta's years.

"Dear Bobbie! Many happy returns of the day!" they cried out together. "Three cheers for Bobbie!"

Roberta was moved, she was close to tears. But before she had time to begin, they were all kissing and hugging her.

"Now," mother said, "have a look at your presents."

They were very nice presents. There was a green and red needle-book, that Phyllis had made for her. Mother had presented her with a silver brooch, shaped like a buttercup, which Roberta had longed for, for years. There was also a pair of blue glass vases from Mrs. Viney. And there were three birthday cards with pretty pictures and wishes.

"Dear, take a look at the table," mother said.

There was a cake on the table covered with white sugar and 'Dear Bobbie' written on it in pink sweets. There were also buns and jam.

"That's my present," Peter said, putting down his much-adored steam engine. It was filled with sweets!

"Oh, Peter!" cried Roberta. "Thank you for your dear little engine that you're so fond of!"

"Oh no," Peter said, promptly, "not the engine, only the sweets."

Roberta couldn't help her face changing a little. She was not disappointed at not getting the engine, rather she felt silly to think of Peter presenting it to her. It now seemed greedy to have expected the engine as well as the sweets. Peter noticed her face change.

He hesitated a minute, then said, "I mean not *all* the engine. I'll let you go halves if you like."

"You're so sweet!" cried Roberta. "It's a splendid present!"

Roberta thought to herself, 'Well, the broken half shall be my half of the engine. I'll get it mended and give it back to Peter on his birthday.'

Chapter 6

Peter's Engine

T he very next morning, Roberta had an opportunity to get Peter's engine repaired, secretly. The opportunity came when Peter and Phyllis went shopping with mother. When they left, Roberta went down to the railway. She went along the line to the end of the platform and hid behind a bush on the other side. She waited patiently till the next train came in and stopped. Then Roberta went across and stood beside the engine. The engine driver and fireman did not notice her. They were leaning out on the other side.

"If you please," Roberta said, but the engine was blowing off steam and her 'please'

was lost in the noise. The only way that she could see to get herself heard, was to climb onto the engine and pull their coats. The step was high, but she managed to climb up and fell on a great heap of coals. Just as she did, the engine driver, who had not noticed her, started the train. By the time she picked herself up, the train had started moving. All sorts of dreadful thoughts came to her. She had read about the express trains that went on for hundreds of miles without stopping. If this was one of them, how would she get back home?

The train was moving faster. She tried to speak, but the men had their backs towards her. Suddenly, she put out her hand and caught hold of the nearest sleeve. The man was startled. They looked at each other in silence for a minute. Then they both broke the silence at the same time.

"You are such a naughty little girl, what are you doing here?" said the fireman. Roberta burst into tears.

Seeing her frightened, they made her sit down on an iron seat in the cab and tried to console her. They silently waited for an explanation while she dried her eyes.

"Please, Mr. Engineer," she said, "I did call out to you from the platform, but you ignored me. I just climbed up to touch you on the arm but then I fell onto the coals. I am so sorry. Please don't be angry!"

She started crying again.

"Of course we are not angry," said the fireman. "But it isn't usual for us to see a little girl tumbling into our coal bunker, is it, Bill? What *did* you do it for?"

"I, too, would like to know that," replied Bill, the engine driver. "What did you do it for?"

Roberta was still crying. The engine driver patted her on the back and said, "Here, cheer up, little girl." "I wanted," Roberta said, "to ask you if you can mend this."

She picked up the brown paper parcel lying somewhere in the heap of coal. She unwrapped the parcel and revealed the toy engine. The driver and the fireman each took the little engine and looked at it.

"I have expertise in driving the engine, not in mending it," said Bill.

"And how will you return to your friends and relations?" inquired the fireman.

"If you'll put me down at the next stop," Roberta said, "and lend me the money for a third-class ticket, I'll get home. I'll pay you back, I promise."

"You're a sweet little lady," said Bill, suddenly changing his tone. "We'll make sure that you reach home safely. And about this engine, Jim, can you use a soldering iron? I think a little bit of it will do the trick."

"Yes, that's what father had said," Roberta explained eagerly.

As her engine was being mended, Roberta began chatting with Jim and learned how a real engine worked. She felt that the three of them were now friends for life. At Stacklepoole Junction, they handed her over to the guard of a returning train, who was a friend of theirs.

She reached home at tea time. "Where have you been?" asked the others.

"To the station, of course," Roberta said.

But she didn't utter a word about her adventure. On the day of Peter's birthday, she mysteriously led them to the station and introduced them to her new friends, Bill and Jim. They handed her the toy engine and it was as good as new.

"Good-bye, oh, good-bye," Roberta said, just before the engine screamed away.

The three children went home up the hill, Peter hugging his engine happily.

Chapter 7

A Stranger

O ne day, mother had gone to Maid Bridge alone and the children were to receive her at the station on her return. They reached the station an hour before the train was to arrive. It was a rainy day and, for July, cold too. They decided to wait on the 'up' side, for the 'down' platform looked very wet indeed.

As they waited, the 'up' train passed by. The children watched its rear lights till it disappeared round the curve of the line and then they turned towards the waiting room. There had been just a few people before, but now they noticed a large crowd on the platform.

"Oh!" cried Peter, with excitement. "Something's happened! Come on!"

They rushed to the place where the crowd had gathered. They could see nothing but the damp backs and elbows of the people on the outer circle of the crowd. Everybody was talking in low whispers. It was evident that something had happened.

Then they heard the firm and official voice of the stationmaster.

"Now, please move aside. I'll attend to this." But the crowd did not move. Then they heard a voice, which thrilled the children. The voice spoke a foreign language. It could have been either French or German.

"It sounds like French to me," said the stationmaster.

"It isn't French!" cried Peter.

"What is it then?" asked more than one voice present in the crowd.

The crowd fell back a little to see who had spoken, and Peter stepped forward.

"I don't know what it is," Peter said, "but it isn't French. I am sure of that."

At last Peter saw the man who was the center of attention. He was a man with long hair and wild eyes, with shabby clothes and

his hands and lips trembled. When he saw Peter, he tried to talk to him.

"Why don't you try speaking French with him?" said a farmer from the crowd.

"*Parlay voo Frongsay?*" began Peter, boldly.

The man with the wild eyes came away from the wall he had been leaning against and sprang forward to take Peter's hands. He began to pour forth a flood of words that Peter could not understand but thought he recognized.

"There!" he said. "*That's* French."

"What does he say?" asked the stationmaster.

"I don't know," Peter was obliged to admit.

"Here," said the stationmaster again, "I'll look into the case."

As the crowd moved away, Phyllis and Roberta joined Peter, who was standing near the man. Peter shook the man's hands warmly and looked at him as kindly as he could.

"Can't you take him into your room?" Roberta whispered to the stationmaster. "Mother speaks excellent French. She'll be here soon, on the next train."

The stationmaster took the arm of the stranger; this time not unkindly. Roberta and Phyllis took hold of his hand and explained in whatever little French they knew, that their mother would soon be there to help him.

Once inside the stationmaster's room, Peter had an idea. He pulled an envelope out of his pocket, which was full of foreign stamps. "Look here," he said, "let's show him these."

They showed him an Italian stamp, and pointing at it made signs of question with their eyebrows. He shook his head. Then they showed him a Norwegian stamp, the common blue kind, and again he shook his head. Then he took the envelope from Peter's hand and searched among the stamps with a trembling hand. At last he pointed to a Russian stamp.

"He's Russian!" cried Peter.

At this very moment, the train from Maid Bridge was signaled.

"I'll accompany him till you bring mother in," said Roberta.

Bobbie was still holding the stranger's hand when Peter, Phyllis and the station-master returned with mother. The Russian rose and bowed ceremoniously. Then mother spoke in French, and he replied, haltingly at first, but then fluently.

"Well, Ma'am, what's it all about?" inquired the stationmaster.

"Oh," mother said, "it's all right. He's a Russian and he's lost his ticket. I'm afraid he's very ill. I think he should stay with us till he gains his health. If you don't mind, I'll take him home with me now. He's a great man in his own country. He writes books, beautiful books; I've read some of them. I'll tell you all about it tomorrow."

She spoke again in French to the Russian and everyone noticed the pleasure and

gratitude in his eyes. He got up and bowed politely to the stationmaster and the children left with them.

"Girls, run home and light a fire in the sitting room," mother said. "Peter run and fetch the doctor."

But it was Roberta who went for the doctor.

"I hate to tell you," she said to the doctor, "but mother has brought home a Russian, who is ill. We found him at the station and I believe he, too, won't have money to pay the bills."

Then, Roberta narrated the whole story to the doctor. When Roberta and the doctor reached the Three Chimneys, the Russian was sitting in the armchair in front of the fire, sipping tea.

"The man seems worn out in mind and body," the doctor said. "The cough's bad, but it's nothing that cannot be cured. He ought to go straight to bed, and let him have a fire at night."

Mother prepared the bed for the Russian and gave him father's clothes to wear. When Roberta came in with more wood for the fire, she recognized the nightshirt the man was wearing. She also noticed the trunk filled with father's clothes lying on the floor. 'Then father hasn't taken his clothes with him!' Roberta thought.

Roberta slipped from the room, her heart beating like a hammer. Why hadn't father taken his clothes? She did not know what to make of it.

When mother came out of the room, Bobbie flung herself at her, tightly clasping her arms around mother's waist, and whispered,

"Mother, Daddy isn't, isn't *dead, is he?*"

"No my darling! How did this thought enter your mind?"

"I, I don't know," Roberta said.

Mother gave her a warm hug.

"Daddy was *quite, quite* well when I heard from him last," she said, "and he'll come back to us some day."

Later on, when the Russian had settled perfectly in the house, mother came into the girls' room. She had to sleep in Phyllis' bed, and Phyllis was to have a mattress on the floor, a most amusing adventure for Phyllis.

As Mother entered the room, two figures wrapped in white sheets rushed towards her. Eagerly they asked, "Now, mother, tell us all about the Russian gentleman." Then came Peter, dragging his quilt behind him like the tail of a white peacock.

"I'm very tired," mother said.

Roberta knew by her voice that mother had been crying, but the others didn't know, so they insisted on the story.

"Well, it's a story long enough to make a whole book. He's a writer and has written beautiful books. In Russia, at the time of the Czar, no one dared to say anything about the rich people doing wrong. If anyone did, they were sent to prison."

"But how can they do this?, "Peter said. "People go to prison only when they've done something wrong." Mother replied, "Yes, that's so in England, but in Russia things are different. I've read the book for which he was sent to prison. For three years he was all alone, kept in a dreadful dungeon, with hardly any light."

Mother's voice choked suddenly, but she continued. "Well, when he was found guilty, he was sent to Siberia. After a few years, he was sent to the mines and was condemned to stay there for life, just for writing a good, noble, splendid book."

"How did he get away?" asked Peter.

"When the war started, some of the Russian prisoners were allowed to volunteer as soldiers. So he volunteered. But he deserted at the first chance he got. While he was in the mines, some friends managed to send a message to him that his wife and children had escaped and come to England. He has come here to find them."

"Does he have their address?" asked Peter.

"No, he just knows that they are in England. He was going to London, when he found that he'd lost his ticket, as well as his purse."

"Oh, do you think he'll find them? I mean his wife and children."

"I hope so. Oh, I hope and pray that he finds his family again," replied mother

Even Phyllis now perceived that mother's voice was very shaky. "Why, mother," she said, "you look troubled; what's the matter?"

Mother didn't answer for a minute.

Then she said, "Dears, when you say your prayers, ask God to show mercy on all prisoners and captives."

"To show mercy," Roberta repeated slowly, "upon all prisoners and captives. Is that right, mother?"

"Yes," mother said, "upon all prisoners and captives."

Chapter 8

The Valiant Rescue

T he Russian gentleman soon regained his health and on the third day he was well enough to come into the garden. A basket chair was put out for him and he sat there, dressed in father's clothes that were too big for him. All the signs of tiredness had vanished from his face. He smiled at the children whenever he saw them. They, too, tried their best to make him feel happy.

Mother wrote letters to several people to find the whereabouts of the Russian gentleman's family. She wrote to members of parliament and editors of papers and secretaries of societies in the hope of finding something.

One day, Phyllis had an idea. She asked the others, "Do you remember Perks, the porter, promising me the very first strawberries out of his own garden? Well, I think they would be ripe by now. Let's go down and see."

Peter and Roberta thought that their visit would surprise Perks and with this belief they went to the station. They had not been there for the last few days.

They found Perks busy reading his newspaper. He greeted them coldly and went on reading the paper. The children could not understand the reason for such a cold welcome. Finally, a long, uncomfortable silence was finally broken, after a lot of coaxing from the children.

Perks was angry with the children, as he felt they had neglected to tell him the story of the Russian. When he learnt the whole story, he returned to his old cheerful self and asked them to come over with him to check the strawberries. "If there are any ripe ones, and you do give them to me," Phyllis said, "you won't mind if I give them to the poor Russian, *will* you?"

Perks narrowed his eyes and then raised his eyebrows. "So, you have not come here to meet me, but for the strawberries," he said.

This was an embarrassing moment for Phyllis. To say yes would seem rude and greedy, and unkind to Perks. But she knew if she said no, she would feel guilty for telling a lie! "Yes," she said, "it was."

But then once again, Perks addressed his young friends. He said, "I love you for your honesty. I will surely give you any ripe strawberries."

The Russian gentleman was so delighted with the strawberries, that the children racked their brains to find some other surprise for him. The next morning, they emerged with the idea of wild cherries. They knew the cherry trees grew along the rocky face of the cliff, out of which the mouth of the tunnel opened. It was not far from the Three Chimneys.

Near the tunnel was a flight of steps leading down to the line. It was just a series of wooden bars, very steep and narrow, more like a ladder than stairs.

"We'd better get down," Peter said, "I'm sure that it would be quite easy to get the cherries from the side of the steps."

So they went towards the little swing gate at the top of these steps. They were almost at the gate when Roberta said, "Hush! Stop! What's that?"

"Look!" Peter cried. "The trees over there! I can't believe my eyes! They are moving!" The trees he pointed to were those that have rough, gray leaves and white flowers.

"They're moving!" cried Roberta. "Oh look! And so are the others! It's like the woods in 'Macbeth'!"

"It's magic!" Phyllis said, excitedly. "I always knew this railway was enchanted. Let's go home."

It really did seem a little like magic, as all the trees, for about twenty yards of the opposite bank, seemed to be slowly walking down towards the railway line. The children watched breathlessly. Some stones and loose earth fell down and rattled on the railway metals far below.

"It's *all* coming down," Peter tried to say, but his voice came out in a squeak.

Suddenly, rocks and trees, grass and bushes came down with a rushing sound. The entire cliff side slipped right away and fell on the line with a huge crash. A cloud of dust rose up.

"Oh no!" Peter said, awestruck.

"Look what a great mound it's made! It's right across the line!" exclaimed Roberta.

"Yes," Peter said, slowly.

"Yes," he said again, as if he had remembered something. Then he almost screamed, "The 11.29 'down' hasn't gone by yet. We must let them know about the mound, or there'll be a most frightful accident!"

"Let's run," said Roberta and they began to run towards the station.

But Peter cried, "Come back! We don't have much time. If we only had something red," Peter said thoughtfully, "we could go round the corner and wave to the train."

"We will wave, anyway," said Phyllis.

"No, we have waved so often that they will not understand that we are alerting them against a danger. Anyway, let's get down there."

They went down the steep steps. Phyllis was red-faced and sweating with anxiety.

"Oh, how hot I am!" She said. "I wish we hadn't put on our...." She stopped short, and then ended in quite a different tone, "our flannel petticoats!!"

When Roberta heard these words, she stopped in the middle of the steps.

"Oh, yes!" she cried. "They're red! Let's take them off." So, Roberta and Phyllis took off their petticoats and ran along the railway. They reached the corner that hid the mound from the straight line of railway. They made six flags out of the petticoats. Peter took out his small knife and cut the branches of two small plants to make a flagstaff.

They set up two of the flags in heaps of loose stones between the sleepers of the 'down' line. Then Phyllis and Roberta each took another flag, and got ready to wave it as soon as the train came in sight. "I shall have the other two myself," Peter said, "because it was my idea to wave something red."

And so the three stood by the railway line, with their flags in their hands, waiting for the train.

After standing for a long time, Phyllis grew impatient. "I suppose the watch is wrong, and the train's gone by," she said. Roberta, too, began to feel sick with suspense. Her hands grew very cold and trembled at the thought of what might happen if the train crashed in to the mound.

Just then, they heard the distant rumble and hum of the metals, and a puff of white steam showed far away along the stretch of line. "There she is," said Roberta.

"Stand firm," Peter said, "and wave like mad! Don't stand on the line, Roberta!"

The train came rattling along fast, very fast.

"They can't see us! They won't see us! It is no good!" cried Roberta. The two little flags on the line swayed as the train came near. It seemed that the train was faster than ever. It was very near now. "Stand back!" cried Peter, suddenly, and dragged Phyllis back by the arm.

But Roberta cried, "Not yet, not yet!" and waved her two flags right over the line.

The engine looked black and enormous.

"Oh, stop! Stop! Stop!" cried Roberta.

It looked like no one had heard her but the engine slackened swiftly and stopped, just twenty yards from the place where Roberta was waving the flags. She saw the great black engine stop dead, but somehow she could not stop waving the flags. Peter and Phyllis ran to the engine driver, who had, by now, jumped out and told him the whole story. When they turned around, they saw Roberta lying across the line. Her hands were still gripped to the sticks of the little, red, flannel flags. The engine driver picked her up, carried her to the train and laid her on the cushions of a first-class carriage.

"Nothing to worry about, she has fainted due to anxiety," he said, "poor little woman."

They sat by Roberta on the blue cushions and the train ran back. Before it reached their station, Roberta had regained consciousness. When they reached the station, the children were the heroes of the day. The praises they got for their 'prompt action,' 'common sense,' and 'ingenuity' was enough to have turned anybody's head. Phyllis enjoyed herself thoroughly. She had never been a real heroine before and it felt wonderful. Peter's ears got very red, yet he too enjoyed himself. They were on cloud nine, that day.

"You'll hear from the company about this, I expect," said the stationmaster.

The children happily went back to the Three Chimneys.

Chapter 9

Reward and Reunion

A ll mother's letters were answered very politely by the editors and secretaries of the various societies, but none of them could tell her about the Russian's family. Roberta racked her brains to think of some way of helping the Russian gentleman to find them, but could not think of anything.

One morning, not long after the landslide, a letter came. It was addressed to Peter, Roberta and Phyllis. The children were

eager to read the contents of the letter. The letter read,

"Dear Sir and Ladies,

We wish to make a small presentation to you for your courageous and prompt action that prevented a terrible accident. The presentation will take place at the station at three o'clock, on the 30th of this month, if this time and place is convenient to you.

Yours faithfully,

Jabez Inglewood,

Secretary of the Great Northern and Southern Railway Co."

The three children had never felt more proud in their lives. They rushed with the letter to their mother, who was overwhelmed with happiness. "But if the presentation deals with money, you must say thank you, but we'd rather not take it," mother said.

They wrote a reply to their invitation and each made a copy and signed it separately. The threefold letter read,

"Dear Mr. Jabez Inglewood,

Thank you very much. We were not thinking of rewards when we decided to save the train. But we are glad to have received your letter. The time and place you mentioned is quite convenient to us. Thank you once more.

Your affectionate little friends."

When at last—after what seemed like ages—the great day arrived, the three children went down to the station at the proper time. Everything was like a dream to them. They were accompanied by the stationmaster, who led them to the waiting room. The room looked quite different. A carpet had been spread out and the room was beautifully decorated with flowers. Quite a number of people were there besides the porter. They recognized several of the faces of the passengers who had been on the train, on '*the red-flannel-petticoat day.*' Best of all, their own old gentleman was there, and he came forward to shake hands with them. The ceremony began with quite a long speech from the District Superintendent. He said all sorts of nice things about the children's bravery and presence of mind and when he finished, everyone applauded. After him, the old gentleman got up and said some words in their praise. Then he called the children one by one and gave each of them a beautiful gold watch and chain. Inside each watch was engraved the name of the watch's new owner and a message, which read,

"From the Directors of the Northern and Southern Railway, in grateful recognition of the courageous and prompt action which averted an accident in 1905."

After this, Peter made a speech and thanked them for their kind gesture. Soon, the children raced up the hill to the Three Chimneys with their watches held tight in their hands.

"I did want to talk to the old gentleman about something else," Roberta said, almost out of breath once they reached home.

"What did you want to say?" asked Phyllis.

"I'll tell you when the time comes. I haven't thought about it much yet," Roberta said.

So, when she had thought a little more, she wrote a letter. It read,

"My dearest old gentleman,

I really want to ask you something. If you could get out of the train and go by the next, I would be happy. I do not want a *thing*; I only want to talk to you about a prisoner and a captive.

Your loving little friend,
Roberta."

She asked the stationmaster to give the letter to the old gentleman. The next day, she asked Peter and Phyllis to accompany her to the station. She revealed her idea to them as usual and they gave their consent to it. They reached the station just in time to find the gentleman coming forward to meet them.

"Hello," he said, shaking hands with all of them in turn. "This is a great pleasure."

"It was good of you to spare time for us," Roberta said politely.

The old man then took her arm and drew her into the waiting room. Phyllis and Peter followed.

"Well?" the old gentleman said. "What is the matter?"

"Oh, please!" Roberta began.

"Yes?" the old gentleman said.

"What I mean to say…" Roberta started again.

"Say it," he said.

"Well," Roberta said and then came out with the story of the Russian who had written the beautiful book and had been sent to prison and to Siberia just for that.

"What we want more than anything in the world is to find his family for him," she continued, "but we don't know how. But you must be very clever, or you wouldn't be a director of the railway."

"Hum," the old gentleman said, "what did you say the name was, Fryingpansky?"

"No, no," Roberta said earnestly. "I'll write it down for you."

She wrote 'Szezepansky' on a nice little notebook that the old gentleman gave, and said, "That's how you write it. You read it 'Shepansky'."

When the old gentleman read the name, he cried out, "That man! Bless my soul! Why, I've read his book! It's translated into every European language. It really is a fine book. And so your mother took him in like the 'Good Samaritan'. Well, well. I'll tell you something, your mother is a very good woman."

"Of course she is!" Phyllis said, in amazement.

"And you're a very good man," Roberta said, very shyly.

"You flatter me," the old gentleman said, with a smile. "Well then, I'll only say that I'm very glad that you approached me with this matter. And you shouldn't be surprised if I find out something very soon. I know a great many Russians in London, and every Russian knows 'his' name. Now tell me all about yourselves."

But the children did not say anything.

"All right, we'll have an examination," the old gentleman said. "You all sit on the table, and I'll sit on the bench and ask questions."

He did, and out came their names and ages: their father's name and business: how long they had lived at the Three Chimneys and a great deal more. Soon, the next train arrived and it was time for the old gentleman to leave.

About ten days after the meeting in the waiting room, the three children were sitting on the top of the biggest rock, in the field below their house. They were watching the 5.15 steam away from the station along the bottom of the valley. Suddenly, they saw a man getting off at the station. He left the road and opened the gate which led across the fields to the Three Chimneys.

"Who on earth is coming to our house?" Peter cried, scrambling down.

"Let's go and see," Phyllis said.

So they went. When they were near enough, they saw that it was their old gentleman.

"Hello!" shouted the children, waving their hands. "Hello!" replied the old gentleman, waving his hat. Then the three of them ran towards him. When they got to him they hardly had breath left to say, "How do you do?"

"Good news," he said. "I've found your Russian friend's wife and child. Here," he said to Roberta, "you run on and give him the good news. Peter and Phyllis will show me the way."

Roberta ran. She told the great news to mother. As soon as she told it to mother, mother told it to the Russian. The Russian sprang up with a cry that made Roberta's heart leap. It was a cry of love and longing, which she had never heard before. He took mother's hand and kissed it gently and reverently and then, sinking down in his chair, he covered his face with his hands and sobbed. Seeing him thus, mother's eyes were also filled with tears.

It was a time for celebration. Peter ran down to the village for buns and cakes. The girls got tea ready and together they all had a delightful time. Mother thanked the old gentleman for his help. He bowed to her and made his way down the path, leaving them to their rejoicing and celebrations.

Being rewarded with watches had been wonderful, but helping to bring a family together seemed a greater reward to the children.

Chapter 10

Perks' Birthday

I t was the day when the children were taking tea with Mr. Perks in the porter's room.

"Miss, that's a beautiful brooch you have got on," Perks said. "It looks like a real buttercup."

"Yes," Roberta said, glad and flushed by his approval. "I never thought it would be mine, not my very own. Mother gave it to me on my birthday."

"Oh, did you have a birthday?" Perks asked, quite surprised. "Yes," Roberta said. "When is your birthday, Mr. Perks?"

"My birthday?" said Perks, quite taken aback. "I gave up celebrating my birthday long before you were even born."

"But you must have been born sometime," Phyllis said, thoughtfully.

"If you insist, it was thirty-two years ago, on the fifteenth of this month."

"Then why don't you celebrate it?" asked Phyllis. "I've many other things to take care of, besides birthdays," Perks said.

"Oh! But what is more important than a birthday?" Phyllis asked.

"The kids and the Missus," said Perks.

The children walked back home, each of them lost in their thoughts and thinking hard what they could do for Perks on his birthday.

"It's horrid to know that somebody doesn't celebrate his birthday," Roberta said.

The next morning, during breakfast, mother said, "I've sold another story. So today, there'll be buns with tea."

Peter, Phyllis, and Roberta exchanged glances with each other.

Then Roberta said, "Mother, would you mind if we don't have the buns today, but on the fifteenth? That's next Thursday."

"I don't mind when you have them, dear," mother said. "But, are you not feeling well or something?"

"We are fine. On the fifteenth, it's Perks' birthday," Roberta said. "He's thirty-two and he says he doesn't celebrate his birthday any more because he has to take care of his family."

"You mean his wife and children?" mother asked.

"Yes," Phyllis replied.

"We thought we would surprise him with a nice birthday celebration," Peter said.

"Therefore, we agreed that on the next bun-day, we'd ask you if we could celebrate Perk's birthday," Peter said.

"I see. Certainly," mother said.

Then they all decided to make cake for Perks' birthday and to write Perks' other name, Albert, on the cake. They considered the gifts they could give Perks on his birthday.

"There must be lots of people in the village who would like him to celebrate his birthday. Let's go round and ask everybody," suggested Peter. "Mother said we weren't to ask people for things," Roberta said, doubtfully.

"She meant that for us, not for the other people. I'll ask the old gentleman too. You see if I don't," Peter said.

They began with the old lady at the post office, but she said she didn't see why Perks should celebrate his birthday, when many others did not. "No," Roberta said, "I would

like everyone to celebrate their birthdays. But we only know when his is."

"Mine's tomorrow," said the old lady. "No one cares about it, no one even remembers it. Now get along."

So they went. Some people did contribute for Perks' birthday. Peter wrote down the lists of the things that people gave in his little pocket book where he kept the numbers of his engines.

Early next morning, Roberta and Phyllis woke up quite early. They plucked a few roses from the garden and arranged them in to a beautiful bunch. Then, they put it in a basket with the needle-book that Phyllis had made for Roberta on her birthday, and a very pretty blue necktie that had belonged to Phyllis.

Roberta took a piece of paper and wrote, 'For Mrs. Ransom, with love on your birthday.' They carried the basket to the post office and placed it on the counter and left before the old woman came out. Peter did not know of this secret adventure, but the girls told him when it turned out all right.

That morning, Peter told mother of their plans for Perks' birthday.

"There's no harm in it," mother said, "but it depends how you do it. I only hope he won't be offended and think of it as charity."

"Oh, but you know mother, we love him, it's not charity," Phyllis said.

On the fifteenth, the children, with the birthday gifts, went to Perks' place in the evening. His wife greeted them and they all waited for Perks to come home. When he saw them, Perks was very upset at first and thought it was charity. How silly Perks was! But he understood when the children explained everything to him. He was, in fact, quite moved by the love and affection of his little friends.

"I don't know if ever I was happier," he said.

Peter, Phyllis and Roberta were happy to see that their efforts had brought happiness to their friend.

Chapter 11

Daddy's Secret

W hen they had first gone to live at
the Three Chimneys, the children
used to talk a great deal about
their father. But as time passed
by, they began to speak less of him. One
day, when mother was working, Roberta
carried her tea to the big room, which they
also called 'mother's workshop.' "Here's
your tea, mother," said Roberta.

Mother laid down her pen among the
pages that were scattered all over the table,

114

and looked at her and asked, "Bobbie, do you think Peter and Phil are forgetting their father?"

"No," Roberta said, indignantly. "Mother, why do you ask this?" "None of you ever speak of him now," mother replied.

Roberta thought for a moment and said, "We often talk about him amongst ourselves."

"But not to me," mother said, "Why?"

Roberta did not find it easy to answer *why*.

"I..." she said and stopped. She went to the window and looked out.

"Bobbie, come here," said mother.

Roberta obeyed her mother's command.

"Now," mother said, putting her arm round her, "try to tell me, dear."

Roberta was at a loss for words.

"Well then," she said, "we thought you were so unhappy about daddy not being here that it would make things worse to talk about him."

Mother remained quiet. Taking up courage, Roberta asked, in a very soft voice, "Will we always be in such a mess?"

"No," mother said, "the worst will be over when father comes home to us."

"I wish I could make things easier for you," Roberta said.

"Oh, my dear, do you think I haven't noticed how good you've all been, not quarrelling as you did before and all the little kind things you do for me? Now, I must get on with my work; but Bobbie," she said, giving her one last squeeze, "don't say anything to the others as yet."

That evening, instead of reading to the children, mother told them stories of the games she and father used to play when they were young. The children were happy to listen to something about their father, after such a long time. They were very funny stories and the children laughed as they listened.

After they had come to the Three Chimneys, mother had allowed each of them to have a piece of their own garden and they were free to plant whatever they liked in it. Phyllis had planted Mignonette, Nasturtium and Virginia Stock in hers. Peter sowed vegetable seeds in his, carrots, onions and turnips. Roberta planted rosebushes in her garden, but all of their new leaves had withered, because she moved them from the other part of the garden in the month of May, which was not at all the right time of the year for moving roses.

It was the day after mother had praised Roberta and the others for not quarrelling. Roberta was digging up the dead rose plants, while Peter had decided to flatten out all his forts and earthworks with a view to making a model of the railway, tunnels and bridges. Roberta went to dump the dead roses in one corner of the garden. When she came back, Peter had got the rake and was using it busily.

"I was using the rake," Roberta said.

"Well, I'm using it now!" Peter said.

"But I had it first," Roberta said, holding on to its handle.

"Then it's my turn now," Peter said.

And that was how the quarrel began.

"Didn't I say this morning that I needed it Phil?"

Phyllis said she didn't want to be mixed up in their rows.

"I wish I'd had a brother instead of two whiny sisters," Peter said.

"I can't think why little boys were ever invented," shouted Roberta, and just as she said it, she looked up and saw the three long windows of mother's workshop flashing in the red rays of the sun. The sight made her remember those words of praise, '*You don't quarrel like you used to do.*'

"Oh!" cried Roberta, just as if she had been hit.

"What's the matter?" Phyllis asked.

"Take the horrid rake then," Roberta said to Peter.

Saying so, she suddenly loosened her grip on the handle. Peter, who had been holding on to it firmly, fell over backward.

"Serves you right," Roberta said, before she could stop herself. Peter lay still for half a moment; it was long enough to scare her. She got really frightened when he screamed and turned rather pale. He then lay back and began to moan, faintly but steadily. Hearing the cries, Mother looked down from the window, and it wasn't half a minute later that she was in the garden kneeling by Peter's side.

"What happened, Bobbie?" mother asked.

"It's not her fault, it's because of the rake," Phyllis said. "Peter was pulling at it, so was Bobbie, and she let go and he went over."

"Stop screaming, Peter," mother said. "Come, stop at once."

Peter stopped. "Now," mother asked, "are you hurt?" "If he was really hurt, he wouldn't make such a fuss," Roberta said, still trembling with anger.

"I think my foot is broken," Peter said, sulkily, and sat up.

Then he turned quite white. Mother put her arm round him.

"He is hurt," she said, "he has fainted. Here, Roberta, sit down and take his head in your lap."

Then mother undid Peter's boots. As she took the right one off, the blood dripped from his foot onto the ground. When the stocking came off, there were three red wounds in Peter's foot and ankle, where the teeth of the rake had pierced him.

"Run and bring some water," mother said.

Phyllis returned with a basinful of water. Peter did not open his eyes till mother had tied her handkerchief round his foot. Then she and Roberta carried him in and laid him on the brown wooden sofa in the dining room. Phyllis then ran to fetch the doctor. Mother sat by Peter, while Roberta prepared some tea for Peter.

'It's all I can do,' she said to herself.

The doctor came and examined the foot. He bandaged it tightly and said, "Now, do not put it down for at least a week."

"He won't be lame, or have to use crutches or have a lump on his foot, will he?" Roberta asked the doctor anxiously, as he was leaving.

"My Aunt! No!" said Dr. Forrest. "He'll be fine in a fortnight."

When mother had gone to her room and Phyllis was filling the kettle for tea, Peter and Roberta found themselves alone.

"He says you won't be lame or anything," Roberta said, softly.

"Of course I know that, silly," Peter said, very much relieved all the same.

"Oh, Peter, I am so sorry," Roberta said, after a pause.

"That's all right," Peter said, gruffly.

"It was *all* my fault," Roberta said.

"If we hadn't quarreled, it wouldn't have happened. I knew it was wrong to quarrel," continued Roberta.

Peter replied, "You shouldn't be sorry. I am happy that it was not you who was hurt."

And so all the differences were buried.

Peter was tired for many days after that, and the sofa seemed hard and uncomfortable in spite of all the pillows and soft rugs. It was terrible to remain tied to one place. To please him, they moved the settee to the window. From there, Peter could see the smoke of the trains winding along the valley, but he could not see the trains.

During his illness, Peter had many visitors. Mrs. Perks came to inquire about his health. So did the stationmaster and several of the village people. But still Peter felt bored.

"I wish there was something to read," Peter said. "I've read all our books fifty times over."

"I'll go to the doctor," Phyllis said brightly, "he must have some to read."

"I expect his books to be only about diseases and their cure," Peter said.

"Perks has a whole heap of magazines which he gets from the train passengers," Roberta said. "I'll run down and ask him."

When Bobbie ran down to Perks' house, she found him busy cleaning lamps.

"So how's the young gentleman?" he asked.

"Better, thanks," Roberta said, "but he is terribly bored sitting at home. I came to ask if you'd got any magazines you could lend him."

Perks replied that he had given them to someone else, but he did have a lot of illustrated papers.

"I am sure Peter would love them. I'll just wrap them with a bit of paper," said Perks.

Pulling out an old newspaper from the pile, he made a neat parcel of it.

"You're a dear friend," Roberta said.

She took the parcel and started for home.

As she waited at the crossing for a train to pass by, she kept the parcel on the top of the gate. Idly, she looked at the printing on the paper that the parcel was wrapped in. Suddenly, she clutched the parcel tighter and bent her head over it. *It seemed like some horrible dream.* She began to read, but the bottom of the column was torn off and she could read no further!

When Roberta reached home, without talking to anyone, she went to her room and locked the door. Then she undid the parcel and read that printed column again, sitting on the edge of her bed. Her face was pale, and her hands and feet were icy cold. She was not able to believe her eyes. When she had read all there was, she drew a long breath.

"So now I know," she said.

What she had read was titled,

'End of the Trial. Verdict and Sentence!'

The person on trial was her father! The verdict was 'Guilty,' and the sentence was 'FIVE YEARS' PENAL SERVITUDE.'

"Oh, daddy," she whispered, crushing the paper hard, "it's not true. I can't believe it. You could never do such a thing! Never, never, never!"

Suddenly, she heard someone hammering on the door.

"What is it?" Roberta asked.

"It's me," Phyllis' voice came. "Tea's ready and a boy has brought Peter a guinea pig. Come, take a look at it." Roberta thought it best to remain silent, and she went down to tea.

Chapter 12

Paper Chase

obbie was struggling to keep the secret to herself.

When she went down for tea, everyone noticed her red, swollen eyes.

"My darling!" cried mother. "What is the matter? Is everything all right?"

"I have a headache," Roberta said. "I'm all right, really."

Tea was not a cheerful meal. Peter was so distressed by the fact that something unpleasant had happened to Roberta, that he limited his speech to just, "More bread and butter, please."

After what seemed like ages, Roberta managed to be alone with mother in her room. She locked the door and stood quietly.

All through tea she had been thinking of what to say. She had thought that 'I know all,' or 'all is known to me,' or 'the terrible secret is a secret no longer,' would be proper lines to start the conversation.

But now, when mother stood before her, she could not say anything. She ran to mother and, putting her arms round her, began to cry.

"Oh, mummy, oh, mummy, oh, mummy!" was all she could say, over and over again.

Mother held her close and waited. Suddenly, Roberta broke away from her and went to the bed. She pulled out the paper, which she had hidden under the mattress. Holding it out, she pointed to her father's name on the paper, with a shaking finger.

"Oh, Bobbie!" mother cried. "You don't believe it, do you? You don't believe daddy did it!"

"No," Roberta almost shouted.

"You shouldn't believe it," mother said. "It's not true. They've shut him up in prison, but he's done nothing wrong. He's a good and honorable man, he belongs to us. We have to think of that, and trust him."

Again, Roberta clung to her mother, and again only one word came to her, but now that word was 'daddy,' and 'Oh daddy, oh daddy, oh daddy!' again and again.

"Why didn't you tell me, mummy?" she asked presently.

"Are you going to tell the others?" mother asked.

"No."

"Why?"

"You understand why I didn't tell you Bobbie," said mother. "We two must help each other to be brave."

"Yes," Roberta said. "Mother, can you tell me about it? Will it be too much to ask? I want to understand everything."

Then, sitting cuddled up close to her mother, Roberta heard 'all about it.' She heard how those men who came to meet her father that night, had come to arrest him,

charging him with selling state secrets to the
Russians. They accused him of being a spy
and a traitor. Roberta also heard about the
trial and about the evidence letters found in
her father's desk at the office, letters which
convinced the jury of his guilt.

"Someone else did it," mother said, "but
all the evidence was against father."

"Mother, how did the letters get in to
father's desk?"

"The person who put them there was the
real culprit. This man had long wanted to be in
father's post. He was extremely jealous because
everyone thought highly of your father. Your
father never quite trusted that man."

"Couldn't we explain all that to
someone?"

"Nobody will listen," mother said, very
bitterly, "nobody at all. Do you think that
I've not tried everything? We are helpless.
All we can do, you and daddy and I, is to
be brave and patient and..." she spoke very
softly, "to pray."

"Mummy, I do think you're the bravest, as well as the nicest person in the world!" Roberta said.

"We won't talk of all this any more, will we, dear?" mother said. "We must bear it. Now, stop crying. We need some fresh air, let's go out into the garden for a while."

Peter and Phyllis were very gentle and kind to Roberta. They thought it best not to ask her anything just then.

A week later, Roberta's mood was brightened by an idea. She decided to write a letter to the old gentleman. It read,

"My dear friend,

You see what is in this paper. It is not true. Father never did it. Mother says someone put the papers in father's desk. The man who got father's position afterwards was jealous of him all along. Father, too, suspected him. Mother says that nobody believes this truth. You are so good and clever, and you easily found the Russian gentleman's family. If you could find out who was responsible for troubling my father, I'm sure they would let father out of prison.

It is only mother and me who know about it and we cannot do a thing on this matter. Peter and Phil are unaware about the happenings. I'll pray for you twice daily as long as I live, if you'll only try to find out. Imagine how you would feel if it had been your daddy! Oh, please do help me!

With love,

Your affectionate little friend,

Roberta."

She cut the article on her father's trial out of the newspaper, and put it in the envelope with her letter. Then she walked down to the station, but took care to remain unnoticed by the others. She gave the letter to the stationmaster and asked it to be given to the old gentleman.

"Did you hear," Roberta said, once she was home, "there's going to be a paper chase tomorrow. Perks thinks that the hare will go along by the line at first. We might go along the cutting. You can see a long way from there."

The children learnt, from Perks, what a paper chase was all about. Perks told them it was a race, held annually, in which one person, dressed like a hare, runs ahead with a bag full of paper bits. A group of people, the hounds, have to track him down by the bits of paper that he keeps throwing.

The next morning, mother packed their lunch and allowed them out for the day to see the paper chase.

"It's a nice idea to go through the cutting," Peter said. "If we miss the paper chase, we shall at least see the workmen clearing the huge mound of trees and rocks from the railway lines."

When they reached the railway line, they got so absorbed in watching the men clearing the lines with picks and spades that they completely forgot about the paper chase. They jumped when a voice behind them panted, "Let me pass, please."

It was the hare, a big-boned, loose-limbed boy, with dark hair lying flat on a very damp forehead. The children stood back. The hare ran along the line and disappeared into the mouth of the tunnel.

Soon, the children saw around thirty people dressed as hounds following the little white bits of paper left scattered by the hare. They also disappeared into the dark mouth of the tunnel. The last one, in a red jersey, seemed to be extinguished by the darkness, like a candle that is blown out.

"Do you think they'll take a long time to pass through the tunnel?" Peter asked the workmen.

"An hour or more," said one of the workmen, looking up from his digging. "It is difficult to run in the dark without knowing the way. The tunnel takes two or three turns."

"Let's cut across the top and see them come out at the other end," Peter said.

Roberta and Phyllis agreed, so they went. After climbing the steep steps, they stood on the top of the hill, where they had so often wished to be.

"Halt!" cried Peter, and threw himself flat on the grass.

The girls also threw themselves down besides him. It really was an exciting adventure.

"I think that the race is over, I am tired of waiting," Phyllis said after every two minutes and then, suddenly, Peter cried, "Look, here he comes!"

They all leaned over to see the hare come out from the shadow of the tunnel.

"See," Peter said. "What did I tell you? Now, look out for the hounds!"

Soon they saw the hounds coming out in groups of twos, threes, sixes and sevens. They were walking slowly and looked tired.

"There," Roberta said, "that's all, so, what shall we do now?"

"Let us go over to the woods and have lunch," Phyllis said. "We can see them for miles from up there."

"Wait, there is one more to come," Peter said. "Remember the red-jersey hound, he hasn't come out yet." They waited for a long time, but the boy did not appear.

"Oh, let's have lunch," Phyllis said. "I'm so hungry I've got a stomach ache. You must have missed him when he came out with the others."

But Roberta and Peter agreed that they had not seen him coming out of the tunnel.

"Let's get down and wait for him at the mouth of the tunnel," Peter said; "then perhaps we shall see him coming along from the inside."

So they waited for the red hound at the mouth of the tunnel. But there was no sign of him.

"Oh! Please, let's have something to eat," wailed Phyllis. "I shall die of hunger, and then you'll be sorry."

"Give her the sandwiches, for goodness sake," Peter said. "Look here," he added turning to Roberta, "don't you think we should also have one? We may need all our strength. I think that the red-jersey hound has met with an accident."

A tunnel seems quite exciting when you see it from inside a train but it's quite different when you walk into it. Then you see slimy, oozy trickles of water running down the walls and the bricks look dull, sticky and sickly green.

Phyllis was really afraid to enter the tunnel, but upon Peter's insistence she did. It was not yet quite dark in the tunnel when Phyllis caught Roberta's skirt and said, "I want to go home. You know that I am afraid of the dark. I don't care what you say but I won't go any further."

"Don't be a silly cuckoo," Peter said, "I've got a candle and matches."

"Come on," he said, as he lit the candle, "we have to find the red-jersey hound."

So the three walked deeper in to the tunnel. Peter led, holding his candle and shouted, 'Hello!' There was no response, so he walked faster. When the others caught up with him, they saw him looking at a pair of red feet. There, slumped down by the curved, pebbly down-line, was the red–jersey hound. His back was against the wall, his arms hung limply by his sides and his eyes were shut.

"He has fainted," Peter said. "What should we do now?"

"Suppose we splash his face with water. I know we haven't any, but milk's just as wet. We have a whole bottle of it," said Phyllis.

"Yes, you splash his face and I will rub his hands; I have seen people doing that," Peter said.

So Peter rubbed the hands of the hound, while Phyllis splashed milk on his forehead.

All three kept on saying, "Oh, please wake up, speak to me! For my sake, speak!"

Chapter 13

A Hound at Home

I t was really dark in the tunnel. The three children were struggling hard to save the life of the boy, whom they called 'the red hound'. The candle had also burnt down, and now gave only a faint light.

"Oh, *do* look up," Phyllis pleaded. "I believe he's dead."

"Open your eyes," Peter said, and shook the boy by his arm. The boy in the red

jersey heaved a sigh, opened his eyes, but shut them again.

"Thank *God*, he is *alive!*" Phyllis said and began to cry loudly. Hearing her cry, the boy opened his eyes and said, "What's up? I'm all right."

"Have this, you will feel better," Peter said, thrusting the milk bottle into the boy's mouth.

"Please drink it," Roberta said.

So he drank. The three watched him in silence.

After having some milk, he tried to move, but the movement ended in a groan.

"I am not able to move, I think I have broken my leg. It's painful," he said.

"Did you tumble down?" asked Phyllis, sobbing.

"Of course not," said the boy, huffily. "I just tripped on one of those wires. I tried to stand but I couldn't, so I sat down. But how did *you* three get here?"

"We saw you entering the tunnel with the other hounds. All the others made their way out of the tunnel but you were not seen anywhere. So we came to find you," Peter said, with pride.

"Wow! You are brave fellows!" remarked the boy.

"Oh, it's nothing," Peter said, modestly. "Can you try to walk, if we help?"

"I can try," the boy said.

He did try, but he could not walk.

Once more, he lay down and closed his eyes. The others looked at each other by the dim light of the candle.

"What shall we do now?" Peter asked.

Roberta said, "You must go and get help. I will stay with him, Phyllis will accompany you."

"Yes, that's the only thing," Peter said.

"Go on," Roberta said, "and please be quick, for the candle won't burn for long."

"I don't think mother would like me leaving you," Peter said, doubtfully. "Let me stay, while you and Phil go and fetch help."

"No, no," Roberta said. "You and Phil go but lend me your knife. I'll try to get his boot off before he wakes up again. Hurry up!"

Phyllis and Peter hurried away for help. When Roberta saw their dark figures rushing out of the tunnel, she was caught by an odd feeling of having come to the end of everything.

Suddenly she gave herself a little shake.

'Don't be a silly little girl,' she scolded herself.

She fixed the candle on a broken brick near the red-jersey boy's feet. Then she opened Peter's knife. It was always hard to manage; usually, a halfpenny was needed to open it. This time, somehow, she managed to open it with her thumbnail. Then she cut the boy's bootlace, and got the boot off. She tried to pull off his stocking, but his leg was dreadfully swollen, so she cut the stocking down, very slowly and carefully.

When Bobbie saw the condition of the boy's leg, she tried to comfort his foot by placing her white, flannel petticoat under it as a cushion.

'Oh, what useful things flannel petticoats are!' she thought.

Then, she wet her handkerchief with milk and spread it over the swollen leg.

"Ouch! That hurts!" cried the boy, who had regained consciousness.

"Oh no, it will help you, it's cool. What's your name?" Roberta asked.

"Jim."

"Mine's Bobbie."

"Are you alone, weren't there some others with you just now."

"Yes, Peter and Phil, they are my brother and sister. They've gone to bring some help."

"Why didn't you go with the others?"

"We couldn't have left you alone," Roberta said.

"Tell you what, Bobbie," said Jim, "you're a brick!"

He held out his arm and Roberta squeezed his hand.

"I won't shake it," she explained, "because it would shake *you* and that would shake your poor leg and *that* would hurt. Have you got a hanky?"

"Generally, I don't carry one."

He felt in his pocket.

"It must be a miracle! I have one today."

She took it, wet it with milk and put it on his forehead.

"You're a jolly good little nurse," said Jim.

Roberta continued talking to him to take his mind off the pain, but it was very difficult to go on talking in the dark. They had blown out the candle to save it. They kept on waiting for help, in silence, which was broken now and then by a few words like, 'You all right, Bobbie?'

Peter and Phyllis tramped down the tunnel towards the daylight.

"It looks like there is no end to this tunnel," Phyllis said and indeed it did seem very long.

"Don't be disheartened," Peter said. "Everything has an end, and you get to it only if you keep on."

"Look!" he exclaimed suddenly. "There's the end of the tunnel; it looks like a pinhole in a bit of black paper, doesn't it?"

The pinhole soon became large and the children could see the blue sky and the gravel path that lay in front of them. Another twenty steps and they were out in the sunshine with green trees on both sides. Phyllis drew a long breath.

"Now, from where should we seek help? Where is the nearest house? I can't see anything except the trees," Peter said.

"Look, I can see a roof over there!" Phyllis said, pointing down the line.

"That's the signal-box," Peter said, "and you know it's wrong to speak to a signalman when he's on duty."

"We are not doing anything wrong; we are trying to save someone's life. I'm not afraid of doing wrong if it is to help someone," Phyllis retorted. "Come on," she said, and started to run along the line.

So Peter ran too. Both children were hot and breathless by the time they stopped. From the windows of the signal box, they shouted 'help' as loud as their breathless state allowed.

They received no answer.

The children climbed up the signal box, and peeped through the door. They saw the signalman sitting on the chair, his head leaned sideways. He was fast asleep.

"My hat!" cried Peter. "Wake up!"

The signalman did not move. Then Peter sprang forward and shook him. Slowly, after some yawning and stretching, the man woke up. The moment he was awake, he leapt to his feet 'like a mad maniac,' as Phyllis said afterwards, and shouted, "Oh, my heavens, what's the time?"

"Twelve thirteen," Peter said.

And indeed it was, by the white, round-faced clock on the wall of the signal-box.

After taking a look at the clock, the man sprang to the levers, and pulled them. An electric bell tingled, the wires and cranks creaked and then the man threw himself into a chair. He was trembling and drew in large gulps of air.

Then suddenly he cried, "Thank God you came in! Oh, thank..."

Peter quickly interrupted, "Look, we have come here to ask for your help. There's a boy in the tunnel whose leg is broken."

"I have not slept a wink for the last five days," said the man irritably. "Why did he go into the tunnel?"

"Why are you getting angry?" Phyllis said, kindly. "*We* haven't done anything wrong, we are just asking for help."

Then Peter explained how the boy came to be in the tunnel. "Well," the man said, "I don't think I can help you, I can't leave the box."

"You might tell us where to find someone to help us. Is there any house near by?" asked Peter.

"There's Brigden's farm nearby. You will find someone there," he said, pointing to a house in the far distance.

"Well, goodbye then," Peter said and rushed out.

They crossed the fields to reach the farm which the signalman had pointed to.

The farmers readily agreed to help them.

Soon, Peter and Phyllis, together with some farmers, returned to the tunnel to help the injured boy.

Roberta was fast asleep and so was Jim. "Worn out with the pain," the doctor said afterwards.

"Where does he live?" the farmer asked, when Jim had been lifted onto the hurdle.

"In Northumberland," answered Roberta.

"I'm in school at Maid Bridge," said Jim. "I should get back there, somehow."

"I think that first a doctor should examine your leg," said the farmer.

"Oh, bring him up to our house," Roberta said. "It's not far from the road and I'm sure that mother won't mind."

"Will your mother like you bringing home strangers with broken legs?" asked the farmer.

"She brought the poor Russian home herself," Roberta said. "I know she'd say we ought to."

"All right," said the farmer.

"Are you sure your mother won't mind?" whispered Jim.

"I am certain about it," Roberta said.

"Then let's leave for the Three Chimneys," said the farmer.

Meanwhile, mother was writing a story about a duchess, a scheming villain, a secret passage, and a missing will. Suddenly the workroom door burst open; she turned to see Roberta, hatless and red-faced with running.

"Oh mother," she cried, "please come down. We found an injured hound in the tunnel. They are bringing him home."

"They ought to take him to the vet," mother said with a worried frown. "I really can't have a lame dog here."

"He's not a dog, he's a boy who had taken part in the paper chase," Roberta said, between laughing and choking.

"They should have taken him home to his mother."

"His mother's dead," Roberta said, "and his father is in Northumberland. I told him that you will help him. You always want to help everybody."

Mother smiled.

"Oh well," mother said, "we must be with him."

When Jim was carried in, dreadfully white with bluish lips, mother said, "I am glad you brought him here. Now, Jim, let's get you comfortable in bed before the doctor comes!"

And Jim, looking at her kind eyes said, "You are so kind, I hate to give you all this trouble."

"Don't you worry," mother said, "I think it is you who is in the most trouble and in need of our help."

Then she kissed him, just like she did to Peter.

Chapter 14

The Grandfather

T hat day, mother remained busy in nursing Jim and assisting the doctor, therefore she couldn't complete her writing. The children sat in the parlor downstairs and heard the sound of the doctor's boots going backwards and forwards over the bedroom floor.

He finally entered the parlor, looking pleased with himself.

"Well," he said, "it's a nice, clean fracture, so it'll mend in a few weeks, I've no doubt in it. He is a brave young chap." "Now," he continued "I looked in to see if one of you could come with me. There are some things that your mother will want at once. Will you help me, Peter?"

Peter agreed happily and went with the doctor. Once they reached the house, the doctor packed up the things that might be needed by mother for nursing Jim's broken foot.

Next day, early in the morning, Peter went to mother's room.

"May I come in, mother?" Peter asked.

"Yes dear," mother said, absently. "I hope everything is fine and you haven't quarreled with anyone."

She wrote a few more words and then laid down her pen and began to fold up what she had written.

"I have just completed a letter to Jim's grandfather. He lives near by, you know."

"I wanted to talk to you about that. Oh Mother, is it necessary to write to him?

Can't we keep Jim and not say anything to his people till he's well? It will be a surprise for them."

"Well, yes," mother said, laughing, "I think...."

"You see," Peter went on, "the girls are all right, and I am not saying anything against them. But it would be really nice if I had a boy to talk to."

"Yes," mother said, "I know it's dull for you, dear. But I can't help it. Next year perhaps I can send you to school. I hope you will like that."

"Mother, I miss my friends," Peter confessed, "but if Jim could stay on after he gets well, we would have a great time."

"I am sure, you would," mother said. "He could stay with us, but you know dear, we're not rich. I can't provide him with the things he desires. And he must have a nurse."

"Can't you nurse him, mother? You nurse me when I get ill."

"That's a pretty compliment Peter, but I can't do nursing and my writing as well."

"Then you *must* write to Jim's grandfather," said Peter. "But mother, I think that his grandfather must be rich enough to pay for a nurse. Grandfathers in books always have a lot of money."

"Well, this is not a book," mother said, "and it is not right to expect something in return for helping someone."

"I say," Peter said, musingly, "it would have been great fun if we all were the characters in your book. Then, you could have made all wonderful things happen. Jim's legs would have been well at once and father would have returned home."

"Do you miss your father very much?" mother asked.

Peter thought she spoke rather coldly.

"Awfully," Peter replied.

Mother was enveloping and addressing the second letter.

Peter went on slowly, "You see, it's not just about missing father, but in his absence there is no other man in the house. It would be so nice if you could write such a book and make daddy come home soon!"

Mother was moved by Peter's words; she put her arm round him and hugged him in silence for a minute.

Then she said, "Don't you think it's rather nice that we're in a book that God is writing? If I were writing the book, I might make mistakes. But God knows how to make the story end just right in the way that's best for all of us."

After breakfast, there was a knock at the door. In honor of Jim's visit, the children were busy cleaning the brass candlesticks.

"It must be the doctor," mother said. "I'll go and look. Shut the kitchen door and, for heaven's sake, don't come out. You all look a sight!"

They knew by the voice and also by the sound of the boots that it wasn't the doctor. But everyone was certain that they had heard the voice before. There was a long interval.

"Who can it possibly be?" Roberta asked.

"Listen, the door is opening. They are coming down; let's peep through the door," Peter said.

These naughty thoughts were racing through their mind, when they heard mother's voice.

"Bobbie," mother called. They opened the kitchen door, and mother leaned over the stair railing.

"Jim's grandfather has come," she said. "All of you wash your hands and faces, then come up and meet him. He desires to meet you all."

The bedroom door shut again.

"Let's have some hot water, Mrs. Viney. I'm as black as your hat," Peter said.

It would be true to say that they were looking as black as coal!

They were busy cleaning themselves, when they heard the boots and the voice come down the stairs and go into the dining room.

After dressing up nicely, they went to the dining room. Mother was sitting on the window seat. But they were surprised to see their old gentleman sitting in the leather covered armchair in which father used to sit.

"Well, I never expected that it would be you!" Peter said, "How do you do?"

Phyllis, who entered the room after Peter, was so happy to see the old gentleman that she cried, "It's our own old gentleman!"

"Oh, it's you!" Roberta exclaimed.

But when they saw mother glancing at them with a strange expression, they remembered their manners.

Together they greeted him, "How do you do?"

"This is Jim's grandfather," mother said.

"How nice!" Peter said with excitement. "It all seems so perfect, just like in those splendid books, isn't it, mother?"

"It is, rather," mother said, smiling. "Things do happen in real life, which resemble the happenings of a book."

"I hope," Peter said, "you're not going to take Jim away, are you?"

"Not at present," the old gentleman said. "Your mother wants him to stay here, it's extremely kind of her. I thought of sending a nurse, but your mother is good enough to say that she will nurse him herself."

"But how will you manage to write?" Peter said, before anyone could stop him. "There won't be anything to eat if mother doesn't write."

"That's all right," mother said, hastily.

The old gentleman looked very kindly at mother.

"Your mother, my dear, has accepted the proposal of becoming a matron at my hospital. That's why she has decided to give up writing for a while."

"Oh!" Phyllis said, blankly. "And shall we have to go away from the Three Chimneys and the railway and everything?"

"No, no, darling," mother said, hurriedly.

"The hospital is called Three Chimneys Hospital," the old gentleman said. "My little Jim is the only patient, and I hope he'll continue to be so. Your mother will be matron, and there'll be hospital staff of a housemaid and a cook, till Jim gets well."

"And after that will mother start writing again?" asked Peter.

"We shall see," the old gentleman said, with a slight, swift glance at Roberta. "Perhaps something nice may happen and she won't have to. One can never say what's in store for the next moment."

The old gentleman rose to leave.

"Mother, I'm so glad you have fulfilled my wish by allowing Jim to stay," said Peter.

"Take care of your mother, my dears. She's one in a million. God bless her," the old gentleman said, taking both of mother's hands, "God bless her! Dear me, where's my hat?" he said. "Roberta, can you come with me to the gate?"

When they reached the gate, he stopped and said, "Child, I got your letter but it wasn't needed. I had read about your father's case in the papers, when it first happened. At that time itself, I had my doubts. And ever since I've known who you are, I have been trying to find out the truth, though I haven't had much success. But I have hopes, my dear, I have hopes."

"Oh!" Roberta said, choking a little. "I know you can do it. You don't think father did it, do you?"

"My dear," he said, "I'm sure that your father is innocent."

Chapter 15

The Joyful Ending!

T he old gentleman's visit, as Jim's grandfather, changed life at the Three Chimneys. The cook, Clara, and the housemaid, Ethelwyn, told mother they didn't need Mrs. Viney. So, Mrs. Viney came only two days a week to do washing and ironing. They even asked the children not to interfere in their work. This gave the children a lot of time to play. As mother had stopped writing, it meant that it was time for lessons.

Though the lessons were nice, they were not as interesting as peeling the potatoes or lighting a fire. Now, if mother had time for lessons, she also had time for play. She also started making little rhymes for the children as she used to do, before father went away.

As far as the lessons were concerned, there was a particular pattern. Whatever the children did, they always wanted to do something else. Roberta would prefer arithmetic to history. When Peter was doing his Latin, he thought it would be nice to be learning history, like Roberta. Phyllis, of course, thought Latin was the most interesting kind of lesson. And so on.

When Jim's foot got better, the children had a pleasant time sitting with him and hearing the tales of his school. Peter listened to all this with immense pleasure.

Mother wrote a poem for Jim. He couldn't understand how mother could write such beautiful poems. Jim taught Peter to play chess and draughts and dominoes; altogether it was a wonderful time for the children.

When Jim's foot was completely healed, Roberta and Phil decided to do something different for him. They racked their brains but couldn't think of anything. "Things do happen by themselves sometimes, without you making them," Phyllis said, as if she was the one who made the world move.

"I wish for something to happen, something wonderful," Roberta said, dreamily.

Roberta's wish was fulfilled, as something wonderful happened exactly four days later.

They were so busy with their lessons and with Jim that they didn't find time to visit the railway. These days, they hardly seemed to be railway children. As the days went by, each had an uneasy feeling about this, which Phyllis expressed one day.

"I wonder if the railway misses us!" she said, sadly. "It seems quite a long time since we have been there."

"It seems ungrateful of us," Roberta said. "We loved it so much when we hadn't anyone else to play with. The thing which troubles me most," Roberta said, "is our having stopped waving to the 9.15 and sending our love to father by it."

"Let's begin it again," Phyllis said.

And they did.

It was September, the grass on the slope to the railway was dry and crisp.

"Run fast," Peter said, "or we shall miss the 9.15!"

"I can't run faster than this," Phyllis said. "Oh! My bootlace has come undone again!"

"Even when you will be getting married," Peter said, "your bootlace will come undone while going up the church aisle. The man you're going to get married to, will tumble over it and smash his nose in. Then you'll say you won't marry him and you'll have to be an old maid."

"I won't," Phyllis said, tartly. "I would rather marry a man with a smashed nose than die as old maid."

"Look! The signal is down. We must run faster!" cried Peter.

They ran. Having not done so for a long time, they once again waved their handkerchiefs to the 9.15.

"Take our love to father!" cried Roberta.

Peter and Phyllis, too, shouted, "Take our love to father!"

As usual, the old gentleman waved from his carriage window but what was remarkable was that from every window, handkerchiefs fluttered, newspapers signaled and hands waved wildly. The train passed by and the children were left looking at each other.

"*Well!*" Peter said.

"*Well!*" Roberta said.

"*Well!*" Phyllis said.

"What does all this mean? I have never seen people waving at us like that!" said Peter.

"I don't know," Roberta said.

"Perhaps the old gentleman told the people at the station to look out for us and wave. He knew we would like it!" said Peter.

Peter's prediction was right; it was all the old gentleman's doing. The old gentleman, who was very well known and respected at this particular station, had got there early that morning. He had waited at the door and said something to every single passenger who passed through. The passengers listened carefully to what the old gentleman said.

Together all of them had soon formed a network. Some read "the news" and passed it on to others. They were all astonished but pleased. When the train passed by the fence, they were ready to wave to the children with their newspapers and handkerchiefs.

"I think they were trying to tell us something important through the newspaper," said Roberta.

"Tell what?" asked Peter.

"I don't know," Roberta answered, "but I feel awfully funny. I feel as if something is going to happen."

They returned home for their lessons. I don't know why but Roberta found it difficult to concentrate on her lessons that day.

"Are you not well, dear?" mother asked.

"I don't know how I feel. Mother, will you let me off my lessons today? I just want to be alone by myself," replied Roberta.

"Yes, of course I'll let you off," mother said. "But what is it, my dear? Are you feeling ill?"

"I don't know," Roberta answered, a little breathlessly. "My head feels all silly and my insides all squirmy and twisty. I think I would feel better in the garden," she said.

But that day, Roberta could not stay in the garden either. It was one of those shiny autumn days, when everything does seem to be waiting. Roberta could not wait.

'I'll go down to the station,' she thought, 'and talk to Perks. I will feel better then.'

So she went down. On the way she passed the old lady from the post office, who gave her a kiss and a hug.

"Oh!" Roberta said to herself, and her heart quickened its beats. "I don't know why but I feel that something is going to happen! I hope it's good."

At the station, the stationmaster was unusually warm in his greetings. Filled with happiness, he hugged Roberta. But he gave her no reason for this unusually enthusiastic greeting.

He only said, "The 11.54's a bit late, miss," and went away quickly to his office.

Perks did not appear until the 11.54 was signaled, and like everybody else, he was holding a newspaper in his hand.

"Hello!" he said. "Here you are. Well, if this is the train, it'll be smart work! Well, God bless you, my dear! I saw it in the paper and I don't think I was ever so glad of anything!"

"What did you see in the paper?" asked Roberta. But already the 11.54 was steaming into the station and at that moment the stationmaster called Perks. Roberta was left standing alone, the station cat watching her from under the bench with his friendly golden eyes.

That day, only three people got off the 11.54. The first one to come out was a countryman with two baskets and a box full of live chickens; the second was Miss Peckitt, the grocer's wife's cousin, with a tin box and three brown-paper parcels and the third one ......

"Oh! My daddy, my daddy!" Roberta cried.

Hearing this cry of joy, everyone in the train put their heads out of the window. Their hearts were moved to see a little girl clinging to a tall pale man. The arms of the man were wrapped around the little girl. In short, it was a very, very happy reunion.

"I knew that something was going to happen," Roberta said, as they went up the road, "but I never thought that it would be so wonderful. Oh, daddy, my daddy!"

"Didn't mother receive my letter?" father asked.

"There weren't any letters this morning."

"You must go in Bobbie, and tell mother, quietly, that everything is fine now. They've caught the man who did it. Everyone knows now that it wasn't your daddy."

"I knew that my daddy couldn't do anything wrong. I always knew it," Roberta said. "Mother and our old gentleman also had faith in you."

"Yes," he said, "I will always be grateful to the old gentleman; it's because of him that I am free. One of your mother's letters told me that you had discovered what was going on. You are very brave Bobbie, I am happy that you became a strong pillar of support for your mother. My little girl!"

They paused for a second.

Roberta decided to surprise the family. So, she asked daddy to stand outside the nearest door. She entered the house and tried to keep her eyes from speaking before her lips had found the right words to break the happy news to mother. She cried out "FATHER HAS COME HOME!" Everyone looked amazed. Roberta's voice called out, "Come in, come in!" The rest of the family gaped in surprise. Once again the family was together! It was just as mother had said; "God knows how to make the story end perfectly, in the way that's best for us all."

THE END